1000527

THE STRANGE CASE OF DR. JEKYLL AND MR. HYDE

With a discussion of MODERATION

www.readingchallenge.com

a division of
Learning Challenge, Inc.
569 Boylston Street
Boston, MA 02116

Manufactured in Canada

0104-1SO

Cover illustration by Richard Martin

Library of Congress Cataloging-in-Publication Data

Savran, Stacy.
The strange case of Dr. Jekyll and Mr. Hyde: with a discussion of moderation / by Robert Louis Stevenson; adapted by
Stacy Savran; illustrated by Eva Clift.
p. cm. — (Values in action illustrated classics)
Summary: A simplified, abridged version of classic about the scientist who drinks a potion that he has created and
becomes a murderous monster, accompanied by a short biography of Robert Louis Stevenson and an essay
focusing on the story's lesson on moderation.
ISBN 1-59203-053-X (hardcover)
[1. Horror stories. 2. Moderation—Fiction.] I. Clift, Eva, ill. II. Stevenson, Robert Louis, 1850-1894. Strange case of Dr.
Jekyll and Mr. Hyde. III. Title. IV. Series.
PZ7.S2672St 2003
[Fic]—dc21   2003009201

THE STRANGE CASE OF
DR. JEKYLL
AND MR. HYDE

by
Robert Louis Stevenson

With a discussion of
MODERATION

Adapted by
Stacy Savran

Illustrated by
Eva Clift

Reading
CHALLENGE®

Dear Parents and Educators:

Reading Challenge® is pleased to introduce a new Literacy and Character Education program—**Values in Action® Illustrated Classics.**

These adapted, timeless tales are perfect for classroom study, homeschooling, and supplemental reading. The stories foster an appreciation of important values that form the basis of sound character education. In addition, each book contains a value-discussion section, a glossary/pronunciation guide, and a short biography of the author.

A full list of **Values in Action Illustrated Classics** available through Reading Challenge can be found at the back of each book.

"Open a book . . . and the world opens to you."

The Editors
Reading Challenge

A division of Learning Challenge, Inc.
www.learningchallenge.com

Moderation in Action

How *The Strange Case of Dr. Jekyll and Mr. Hyde* Illustrates the Value of Moderation

Moderation is knowing how much is too much and how little is too little. Showing moderation is choosing the middle between two extremes.

For instance, imagine that you have a difficult test tomorrow. You want to get an A, so you work out study plans. Plan 1 is to not study at all and hope that you get an A. Plan 2 is to study all night long, without taking a break for sleep or food. Plan 3 is to study after school and then after dinner. You may even ask a parent to help you.

Which plan is most likely to work? Plan 1 won't work. How can you succeed if you don't even try? Plan 2 won't work either. You will be so tired from studying, you won't be able to concentrate on the test! Plan 3 is a more moderate, realistic plan. It is the best choice. You will have time to sleep well, but you also will get your studying finished. Asking someone for help will also help you stay focused.

In *The Strange Case of Dr. Jekyll and Mr. Hyde*, Dr. Henry Jekyll loses track of how much is too much. He starts working on a series of experiments. When the experiments succeed, he becomes very involved in them. We can all understand his excitement. However, Dr. Jekyll becomes so involved in his work that he forgets other, more important things in life. He loses sight of the need for moderation. Instead of limiting his time doing experiments in order to keep living his life, he spends *all* of his time absorbed in his lab. He cuts himself off from his friends and the people who care about him. The result is disaster.

At the end of the story, Dr. Jekyll realizes that he has been working to an extreme degree. The effects of his experiments are dangerous to his health and well-being. He realizes that by practicing moderation, he could regain his health and reconnect with the friends he's ignored. But Dr. Jekyll is afraid that it is too late.

This is an important lesson about moderation. If we are able to recognize when we have gone too far, we can learn from the mistake and approach things differently next time.

Contents

Chapter 1

BLACKMAIL
HOUSE

$\mathcal{M}$r. Gabriel John Utterson was a man of few words and rare smiles. One would surely think that such an unfriendly person would have no friends. Oddly enough, however, Mr. Utterson kept a close-knit circle of friends who were quite at ease with him. They found him to be accepting of others' mistakes. In many cases, he was willing to help the wrongdoer. He was never one to criticize.

Mr. Utterson was a lawyer. He counted as friends his relatives and other people he had known for a long time. So it was that Mr. Richard Enfield, a well-known man about town, was both Mr. Utterson's cousin and friend.

Each Sunday, the two friends walked around the city of London. People who saw them reported that not a word would pass between the two. One would look as bored as the other! Yet the lawyer and his young cousin continued to take these walks. They even avoided business calls so that they would not be interrupted. Why they did it remained a mystery to all who saw them.

It was on one of these silent Sunday walks that the lawyer and his cousin found themselves on a quiet side street in a busy part of London. The street was unlike the others in its dingy neighborhood. With freshly painted window frames and general cleanliness, it was a welcome sight.

Upon nearing the corner, the two men came across an old, two-story building with no windows. Its cracked

and filthy walls made it clear that no one was taking care of it. It looked almost evil in its surroundings. The pair stopped and stared. Neither man was able to take his eyes off it.

Mr. Enfield lifted his walking cane and pointed it toward the building's battered door. "Have you ever seen that door?" he asked Mr. Utterson, as a sudden look of horror flashed across his face.

"Indeed I have," replied Mr. Utterson, "but to me it is just a door. I can see by the look on your face that it means a great deal more than that to you."

"Oh yes! One frightful night, I met that door, my good man," Mr. Enfield said quietly.

Mr. Utterson's usually careless tone took on a note of curiosity. "Please, go on," he said. He knew that something terrible must have happened to have upset his young cousin so.

Glancing over his shoulder to make

sure that they were alone, Mr. Enfield began his tale. "Well, it was like this," he whispered. "I was walking home from a party very late one evening. The streets were empty of people, but full of lamps flooding with light. Everyone, or almost everyone, was asleep in their beds.

"As I neared a corner not far from here," Mr. Enfield went on, "I saw a little man stomping down the sidewalk across the street. At the same moment, I saw a young girl of eight or nine come running as hard as she could down the other street. Where either of them was racing to at that hour I cannot imagine, but fate stepped in their tracks. The two ran right into each other at the corner. The poor child was knocked to the ground."

The lawyer shook his head in disbelief. "Dear, oh dear," he said. "But how is that accident connected to that door?"

"You will understand in a moment. I am just getting to the real tragedy,"

said Mr. Enfield. "The man had the wind knocked out of him, but was still standing. He just trampled over the fallen girl's body and began to run away as she screamed!"

Completely shocked and at a loss for words, Mr. Utterson turned quite pale. He felt as if he had been knocked off his own feet.

Mr. Enfield went on. "I instantly called out and chased the villain. When I caught up with him, I grabbed his collar and dragged him back to where the child still lay on the ground. A group of people had already gathered, including the girl's family and a doctor who had been called to the scene. The trampled child turned out to be more frightened than hurt, thank heavens. Still, the group of us was not about to let the stranger get away unpunished.

"There was something odd about our reactions to this man," Mr. Enfield said thoughtfully, with a finger on his chin. "It is certainly natural to hate a man like this. But there was something else going on that I can't quite figure out. I had taken a dislike to him at first sight, even before what happened at the corner. The doctor, usually in control of his emotions, looked like he was going to rip the stranger to shreds.

"Well, killing him was out of the question, so we did the next best thing. We told the man we would make a scandal out of it. He was beginning to look frightened as our group stood around him. But he managed to keep a dark manner of calm. He was smirking as if he knew something that could keep him out of trouble. I tell you my friend, I saw the devil in this man.

"To keep us from spreading the news, he offered us money," Mr. Enfield went on. "'Name your figure,' he said. We told him that we would accept a hundred pounds for the child's family. He agreed and brought us to the place we are standing in front of right now. He pulled out a key to that door and went inside. He came back quickly with ten pounds in gold and a check for the rest. The check was signed with a well-known, honorable name. It was a name that I dare not mention.

"I wondered if the signature was real or forged by the man. I asked him. I said that it was hard to believe that a man could walk into such a door at four

in the morning and come out with another man's check for almost a hundred pounds. He insisted upon going to the bank with me the next morning to cash the check himself. I was completely shocked to discover that the check was indeed real!"

Mr. Utterson's eyes and mouth were wide with surprise. Mr. Enfield took notice and paused to let his cousin soak in all that he had been telling him. This story was too much for Mr. Utterson to bear! All of his senses seemed to go out of whack. He had to take a deep breath before his cousin could continue.

"I see that you feel as I do," said Mr. Enfield. "This is a bizarre story. I have been going over and over it in my mind. Why would a kind, well-respected member of society hand over a check to this devilish man? So far, the only reason I have come up with is blackmail. Perhaps that honest man was having to pay for some of the mistakes of his youth. Blackmail House is what I call that place with the door now. Though even that," he added, "is far from explaining all."

"Does this well-respected check signer live behind this door?" asked Mr. Utterson.

"No, he doesn't," replied Mr. Enfield. "I noticed a different address for him on the front of the check. Since then, I have studied this strange building for myself. It seems that no one other than the wicked gentleman goes in or out of that door, and that is only once in a while. The chimney is usually smoking, so perhaps somebody does live there. But the buildings are so close to each other here that it's hard to say where one ends and another begins."

Mr. Utterson looked very unhappy. "If you will, my good man," he asked, "please tell me the name of the man who walked over the child."

"I suppose it can do no harm," replied Mr. Enfield. "Just please, let's keep this between ourselves."

The lawyer nodded silently, with a serious look on his face.

"It was a man by the name of Hyde," said his cousin.

Utterson was suddenly aware of a chill in the air. He shivered.

"What does he look like?" he asked.

"Hyde is difficult to describe," said Mr. Enfield. "There is something displeasing, something nasty about him. But I cannot pinpoint it. There is just something not right about him."

"You are sure that he used a key to enter that door?" asked Mr. Utterson.

"Have you any reason to doubt anything I have told you?" said Mr. Enfield, surprised.

"I apologize," said Mr. Utterson. "It is just that right now I am hoping that there has been some mistake. If not, I am certain that I know the name of the person who signed the check."

Standing still and silent for a moment, Mr. Enfield thought over the events he had just described. "I fear that I've been correct in every detail of my story, Cousin," he said.

Mr. Utterson sighed. The two men agreed not to share the story with anyone else. The lawyer did not, however, reveal the name of the person he believed had signed the check. Then the friends shook hands and parted as the sun disappeared below the horizon.

Chapter
2

DR. JEKYLL'S WILL

$\mathcal{M}$r. Utterson returned to his house and sat down to dinner. Although his stomach was empty, his mind was full. He could not eat more than a few bites of his meal. His restless mind then took him into his study. There, he opened his safe and took from it an envelope marked *Dr. Jekyll's Will.*

The lawyer took out the paper and examined it. He was more confused now than when it was first given to him. It plainly stated what to do if Dr. Henry Jekyll died or disappeared or was absent without explanation for longer than three months. Everything that he owned was to be given to to his "friend" Edward Hyde.

"I cannot understand it," Mr. Utterson thought out loud. "What would lead an honest man like Jekyll to design such an odd will? But given what I now know about this devil called Hyde, I can only imagine that he knows some terrible secret that the good doctor wishes to cover up. It must be as I feared! I am sure that Jekyll is the man who signed the check."

With that, the lawyer put the will back in the safe, put on his coat, and left the house. He set off in the direction of Cavendish Square to visit the dependable Dr. Lanyon. "If anyone knows anything when it comes to Dr. Jekyll," thought Utterson, "it is our dear friend Lanyon."

Utterson was greeted by Lanyon's butler and quickly led into the dining room. There, the doctor sat alone with an almost-empty plate in front of him. At the sight of his visitor, the gentleman sprang up from his chair and welcomed him joyfully with both hands. Utterson, Lanyon, and Jekyll were old friends from their college days.

After a little small talk, the lawyer eased into the difficult subject he wished to bring up.

"I suppose, Lanyon," he said, "that you and I must be the two oldest friends that Henry Jekyll has."

"Well, I wish his friends were younger," chuckled Dr. Lanyon. "I suppose we have been his friends the longest. However, I haven't had the pleasure of the good doctor's company lately. Is he well?"

"Oh, well, yes, I suppose the doctor is fine," said Utterson, somewhat surprised. "But what has happened? I would think that two scientists with the same interests would spend a great deal of time together."

"Henry Jekyll has begun to have strange scientific ideas about things," said Lanyon. "I believe that he has gone wrong in the mind—a little loopy, if you know what I mean. Although I do still take an interest in him, for old times' sake."

"Well, have you ever come across a new friend of his—a man called Hyde?" asked Utterson.

"Hyde?" repeated Lanyon. "No. Never heard of him."

That was all the information the lawyer left with that evening. He returned to his house with an uneasy mind. He tossed and turned that night. He had nightmares about his cousin's creepy tale. When the clock struck six the next morning, the lawyer awoke with a strong curiosity. He wanted to see Mr. Hyde for himself.

Chapter 3

HYDE AND SEEK

*F*rom that day forward, whenever he was able, Mr. Utterson began to linger in the shops on the street of Blackmail House. He was waiting to get a good look at the man who had some kind of mysterious power over his unfortunate friend Jekyll.

"We shall play a game of Hyde and Seek!" Utterson had thought, to his own amusement.

At last, his patience was rewarded. One chilly night at ten o'clock, the side street was empty and silent. Mr. Utterson had been leaning in a shop's doorway when he heard footsteps approaching. His heart leaped in his chest. Without thinking, he stepped out onto the street.

He quickly realized that he had just found the man he had been searching for. As the gentleman walked toward him, Utterson saw that he was small and plainly dressed. Even from a distance, though, there was something

about the man that made the lawyer want to look away. Still, he did his best not to.

Then, suddenly, the small man crossed the street. He headed for the battered door and took a key from his pocket. Before he could open the door, Mr. Utterson stepped out of the shadows and touched him on the shoulder.

"Mr. Hyde, I presume?" said Utterson.

Mr. Hyde shrank back in fear. He quickly pulled himself together and answered coldly, "That is my name. What do you want?"

"I see that you are going in," replied the lawyer, staring directly into the devil's face. "I am Mr. Utterson, an

old friend of Dr. Jekyll's. I want to pay him a visit and thought I might be able to go in with you."

"Dr. Jekyll is not in right now. He is away for a while," hissed Hyde. Then he snapped at Utterson, "How did you know my name?"

"Someone described you to me," was the reply.

"Who described me?"

"We have some of the same friends," said the lawyer.

"Who are they?" asked Mr. Hyde, his voice cracking slightly.

"Jekyll, for example."

"You are a liar! He never mentioned me!" cried Hyde, his face flushing red with anger.

"Hush!" said Mr. Utterson. "There is no need to get so upset, Mr. Hyde. I simply—"

The small man interrupted the lawyer with a harsh, evil laugh that pierced the quiet night air like the howl

of a wolf. In the next moment, he swiftly unlocked the door and disappeared inside the house. He slammed the door behind him.

The lawyer stood outside where Mr. Hyde had left him. He was trembling, yet somehow satisfied at having seen the horrible Hyde at last. He began to walk down the street, pausing every step or two to think. Mr. Hyde was short and pale. He seemed deformed somehow, but there were no clear markings. He had spoken with a husky, whispering voice. All of this was plain and true, but could not explain the disgust and fear that Mr. Utterson had felt toward him.

"Perhaps it is his wicked soul that comes to the surface," thought Mr. Utterson aloud. "Oh, my poor Henry Jekyll! I believe I have just met the devil in your new friend!"

The lawyer walked around the corner to a street lined with very old houses. Most of them were home to London's high society. One of the houses belonged to Dr. Henry Jekyll. Mr. Utterson knocked at the door. It was opened by Poole, Jekyll's butler.

"Is Jekyll at home, Poole?" asked the lawyer.

"Please come in and have a seat while I check," answered Poole, leading Mr. Utterson into a large, comfortable den with a fireplace and a sofa. Then the butler left the room.

The lawyer began to get an uneasy feeling. Usually, he was received with a very warm welcome in this room. But tonight, the light from the fire cast strange shadows on the walls. Despite the fire, there also was a chill in the air.

It caused the lawyer to shiver. He was ashamed at the relief he felt when Poole returned to say that Dr. Jekyll had gone out.

The lawyer could not help but ask, "Poole, is it okay for Mr. Hyde to go into that old building around the corner when Dr. Jekyll is away from home?"

"Oh, yes, sir," replied the butler. "By Dr. Jekyll's orders, Mr. Hyde is allowed into the laboratory. He has a key."

"Very well then. Good night, Poole."

"Good night, Mr. Utterson."

The lawyer headed home with a heavy heart. "My poor old friend," he thought. "We all have secrets from our pasts. Some are worse than others, to be sure. Why do *you* deserve this type of punishment? The dreadful Hyde must have some dark secrets of his own, by the looks of him. I imagine that his secrets are far worse than yours. I must find a way to expose the evil man and wreck his power over you. If he knows about your will, he may grow impatient to inherit your wealth! Oh, dear Jekyll, if only you would let me help you. There is no time to waste, for I feel sure that you are in terrible danger!"

Chapter 4

THE PROMISE

*A*s luck would have it, Mr. Utterson soon received an invitation to Dr. Jekyll's home for a dinner party. The lawyer was eager to talk with the doctor about the will, so he stayed behind after the other guests left. The doctor was pleased. He found it comforting to sit with the quiet lawyer before being left alone for the rest of the evening.

Tonight, though, Dr. Jekyll's comfort was disturbed by his friend, who was very talkative.

"I have been wanting to speak to you about your will, Jekyll," began Mr. Utterson.

Quickly changing the subject Jekyll said, "I understand that you paid a visit to our dear friend Lanyon!" Then, more softly, he added, "That foolish coward. Oh, I know that he is a good fellow—you need not frown at me. I just find it silly that he calls himself a scientist. The man doesn't even do experiments! He just accepts what he is given and what he is told. It's very disappointing."

"You know I never approved of the will," Mr. Utterson said, ignoring the doctor and returning to the matter at hand.

"My will? Oh, yes, I know that," said the doctor, shifting uncomfortably in his chair.

"Well, I now know more about your Mr. Hyde. I feel that it is my duty to tell you how upset I am," said Utterson.

The doctor's handsome face grew pale and the light in his eyes vanished.

"I would rather not discuss this with you, Utterson. You would not understand the difficult situation I am in. Believe me, there is nothing you can do to help me with it."

Utterson came back with, "I beg to differ, my good friend! You know that I can be trusted."

"My friend, this is very good of you, and I cannot find the words to thank you. I do trust you completely. But believe me, this is a very private matter. Still, to put your mind at rest, I will swear one thing to you: The moment I choose to, I can be rid of Hyde. I give you my word on that."

"I apologize then, for getting into your business," said the lawyer. "It seems that you have everything under control. At the very least, you do a fine job of pretending that all is well."

"Thank you, my good man," said the doctor, with an obvious sigh of relief. "I really do have a great interest in poor

Hyde. I ask only that you promise me one thing. If I should be taken away in some manner, please make sure that the terms of my will are carried out. If you knew what I do, I think you would do it gladly. It would be a weight off my mind if you would make me this promise."

Utterson looked straight into Dr. Jekyll's dark, pleading eyes and saw a tortured man. Although he knew that he would later regret it, he finally said, "I promise."

Chapter 5

WITNESS
TO A CRIME

Almost a year later, on a clear October night, London was shocked by a horrifying crime. The victim was one of the most respected men in town. The crime's only witness was a young woman who lived alone in a house close to the river. She had been sitting at the window in her second-story bedroom, gazing at the full moon.

Suddenly, the woman was distracted by the sight of a nice-looking older gentleman with white hair. He was approaching a smaller gentleman, to whom she paid less attention at first.

When the men passed right beneath the woman's window, she recognized the small man as Mr. Hyde. He had once visited her boss at work. She recalled feeling the same intense dislike for him then as she felt at this moment.

The old man must have been asking Mr. Hyde for directions, because he was pointing and writing something down. But Hyde appeared impatient. Suddenly, Hyde began swinging his cane wildly. Then, in a fit of rage, he began stamping his feet and carrying on like a madman. The old man stepped back and looked frightened.

The next moment, Hyde hit the poor gentleman with his cane until he fell to the ground. Then Hyde trampled over his victim and ran away. At the horror of these sights and sounds, the woman fainted.

At two o'clock in the morning, the
woman awoke and called for the police.
When she went back to the window, she
saw the old man still lying in the street.
Beside him was part of the wooden cane
that had been Hyde's weapon. When the
police arrived, they found that the victim
was dead. They also found a sealed and

stamped envelope in his coat pocket. It was addressed to Mr. Utterson.

Later that morning, the police took the envelope to the lawyer, who was getting ready to go to work. They told him of the night's awful events. "We are hoping that you can help us identify the victim and lead us to his killer," said Inspector Newcomen.

"Yes, I recognize the poor soul," said Utterson when they arrived at the police station. "I am sorry to say that this is Sir Danvers Carew, the respected politician. He was a client of mine. The envelope held papers relating to legal matters he and I were going to discuss."

The inspector showed Utterson the broken cane and said, "Perhaps you can help us find the man who committed this awful crime."

With one look, Utterson knew that the broken cane was the same one he had given Henry Jekyll as a gift. Jekyll must have passed it on to his new friend Hyde.

"Yes," said the lawyer, feeling sick to his stomach. "I think I can take you to the home of Edward Hyde."

Utterson waved down a cab. He gave the driver directions to a street in Soho, a section of London that was home to crooks of all kinds. As the cab turned onto Bellview Lane, a thick fog lifted, revealing a row of broken-down homes. Once, they had been the estates of wealthy people.

A chill ran up the lawyer's spine as he stepped out of the cab. He knew that evil lurked in every corner of these streets.

Utterson and the police inspector climbed the front steps to a large house with a rusted sign above the door that said THE CHURCHILLS. They were greeted by a sour-faced old woman.

The woman eyed the two suited men suspiciously and said, "What do you want?" The lawyer asked her if Mr.

Hyde lived there. She said that he did, but he very rarely came home. In fact, until yesterday it had been almost two months since she had seen him. Yesterday he was home only for an hour.

"Well then, we wish to see his rooms," said the lawyer. When the woman began to protest, he said, "Maybe you don't

understand. This is Inspector Newcomen of London's police department."

"Aha!" she shouted with shameless delight. "Hyde is in trouble! What has that miserable monster done now?"

The inspector and the lawyer looked at each other. "He is not very popular," said the inspector, "and we have come to find out why that is. Now, my good woman, please let us have a look around the place."

When they finally made it past the woman and went into one of Hyde's rooms, they were surprised to find it decorated in luxury and fine taste. A wine closet stood in one corner, and expensive art hung on the walls. Fine carpets covered the floors. Hyde must have found a sneaky way to take these riches from the good doctor.

They also noticed that the dresser drawers were open and looked as if they had been ransacked. In the small fireplace lay a pile of ashes, as though

papers had been burned. From the ashes, the inspector pulled out the stub end of a checkbook.

Just as they were about to leave, Utterson saw the other half of the cane—the murder weapon—leaning against the door. This was all the proof they needed to connect Hyde to Carew's murder.

The checkbook was not completely burned. They could read enough to

know that a great deal of money was still in Hyde's account. This gave the inspector new hope.

"Now we've got him!" he told Utterson. "Hyde obviously left in a panic, or he wouldn't have burned his checkbook and left the cane behind. He will certainly need this money soon. We shall give the bank a picture of Hyde and ask them to let us know when he comes to collect."

However, the inspector's perfect plan soon fell apart. No photos or family members of Hyde's could be found. When an artist tried to draw Hyde from descriptions given by a few people, he couldn't come up with a good sketch. Each person seemed to be describing someone different. The only thing they agreed on was that Hyde seemed to be deformed somehow. Since no one could be more specific, though, this was of no help to the artist.

Chapter 6

THE LETTER

Later that afternoon, Utterson paid Dr. Jekyll a visit. He was greeted by Poole, who led him out the back door and across a courtyard to a building directly in back of the house. The lawyer recognized the dingy building at once. This was where Hyde had gone to get the suspicious check! Utterson hadn't realized until now that its back entrance was so close to Dr. Jekyll's house.

As he made his way through a dark hallway, he noticed a harsh, sickly smell. When he reached the lab, he saw that every inch of the tables was covered with

bright-colored, sharp-smelling chemicals
in tubes and jars. At the far end of the
room was a stairway.

Poole climbed the stairs with the
lawyer at his heels. He knocked on the
door to Jekyll's office.

"Mr. Utterson to see you, sir," called the butler through the closed door.

"It's open, Poole. Please let my friend in," said the doctor in a weary voice.

There sat Dr. Jekyll by the fire, looking very ill. He did not rise to meet his visitor, but held out an ice-cold hand in welcome. "I'm so glad you came," said the doctor in a strange, cracked voice.

As soon as Poole left them, Utterson said, "So, have you heard the news?"

The doctor shuddered. "I heard them shouting about it in the square," he said. "The murder has created quite a scandal, I suppose?"

"You *suppose*? Of course it has!" said Utterson. "Listen, my dear friend, I know that this Hyde fellow has some sort of hold on you. But please promise me that you have not been crazy enough to hide this man!"

"Utterson, believe me, he does not want my help," said the sad-looking doctor. "He is gone, and gone for good. Mark my words: He will never be heard from again."

"Well, Henry, for your sake, and for the safety of others, I hope you are right. But how can you be so sure?" asked the lawyer, highly doubtful.

"I am quite sure, though I can't tell you why. Please, just put your faith in me, as you have done so many times before," pleaded Dr. Jekyll.

"Are you afraid that telling me the truth will lead to his being caught by the police?" asked the lawyer.

"No," said the doctor. "I don't care anymore what becomes of Hyde. I only wish to protect myself now. I don't want my good name smeared by being connected to this man and his horrible deeds. People will begin to think that I have fallen from grace. I can't let that happen—I will not!" shouted the doctor, shaking his fist in the air. Then, suddenly, a coughing fit came on and Dr. Jekyll was gasping for air.

"Please, my good man!" said Utterson, gently patting the doctor's back. "I beg of you, please calm down. I can see that all this trouble has put a terrible strain on your health. Shall I ask Poole to get you some hot tea?"

"No, thank you," replied the doctor, growing calm again. "I will be just fine soon, you will see. But there is one thing left to discuss with you, my friend. I have received a letter from Hyde. I don't know if I should show it to the police. I would like to leave it with you, Utterson, because I know that you will get it into the right hands."

The lawyer took the letter and studied it carefully. It read:

Dear Dr. Jekyll,
How could I ever repay you for your generosity? I am certainly unworthy of your kindness. I ask only that you do not worry about my safety. I have found an escape. A thousand thanks are not enough.
                              Edward Hyde

The lawyer was very pleased with this letter. Although it didn't reveal where Hyde was, at least it shed some light on the bond between he and Jekyll. Hyde obviously felt very grateful to Jekyll for his great generosity. Utterson was surprised, yet relieved.

However, there was one more thing that still worried the lawyer. "Jekyll, who came up with the terms of your will? Whose idea was it to plan for the possibility of your 'disappearance'?"

The doctor looked as if he were about to faint. The lawyer shook him to keep him from passing out. "It was Hyde's idea," Jekyll mumbled.

"Just as I thought!" exclaimed Utterson. "He was planning to murder you! You have had quite a narrow escape."

"I have had a great deal more than an escape," said the doctor. "I have learned a very precious lesson." Then the doctor turned his face toward the fire. Utterson thought that he could see tears in the doctor's eyes.

The lawyer left as the doctor stared silently into the fire. Yet Jekyll seemed to be much more peaceful and content than when Utterson had first arrived. Utterson hoped that taking the matter of Hyde's letter into his own hands would ease the doctor's worries.

On his way out, Utterson stopped to speak with Poole. He said, "A letter was dropped off here today for Dr. Jekyll. Did you see the person who brought it?

Poole replied that nothing had come except by regular mail, "And nothing very interesting at that," he added.

In that case, thought the lawyer, there were only two ways Jekyll could have come by that letter. Either it had been delivered directly to the laboratory door, or it had been written inside the doctor's office. Could Hyde have visited the lab before he disappeared?

Utterson's first move was to go see his head law clerk, Mr. Guest. Guest was an expert on handwriting. "I have a document here," Utterson told him, "that was written by the murderer of Sir Danvers Carew. It is in his own handwriting."

Guest loved the challenge of a brand-new case. He sat down and studied the letter. "Well, the handwriting is definitely odd, but not one of a madman."

Just then, a servant entered with a note addressed to Mr. Utterson.

"Is that from Dr. Jekyll, sir?" asked the clerk. "I thought I recognized the handwriting. Is it private?"

"Only an invitation to his home for dinner. Why? Would you like to see it?"

"Yes, if I may," replied Guest. Then he laid the two sheets of paper alongside

one another and stared silently at them for a few moments.

"Why are you comparing *these* two notes, Guest?" Utterson finally asked.

"Well, sir," said the clerk, his eyes shining with the thrill of discovery, "Look! The two hands are very similar.

The only real difference is in the way the letters are sloped."

Mr. Utterson put his hand to his collar, for suddenly it seemed too tight. He felt as if he were choking. He loosened his tie and cleared his throat.

"I must ask you not to speak of this to anyone," said Utterson to his clerk.

"I understand, sir," said Mr. Guest.

Later, alone in his study, Mr. Utterson locked Hyde's note into his safe. "What the devil is going on here?" he thought, running a hand through his hair. "Henry Jekyll has forged a letter to protect a murderer!" Utterson's blood ran cold in his veins.

Chapter 7

RAT FOOD

$\mathcal{T}$he hunt for Hyde continued. Thousands of pounds were offered in reward for his location. As the days passed, Mr. Utterson grew more deeply relieved that Hyde could not be found. He still felt grief over the death of Sir Danvers Carew. But that grief was soothed by the murderer's disappearance.

For Jekyll, having that evil man out of his life made all the difference. Soon he was out and about, his health greatly improved. For more than two months, he seemed at peace.

During this time, Utterson was

invited more than once to the doctor's home for dinner parties. The usual circle of friends was there, including Dr. Lanyon. It felt just like the old days—the sunny doctor displaying his warm charm and generosity.

Then, in mid-January, Utterson made a spur-of-the-moment visit to Jekyll's home. To his surprise, he was not invited inside. Disappointed by this unexpected treatment, he asked Poole for an explanation. "The doctor is staying in the house," said the butler, "and will see no one." Then he shut the door.

Three days later, the lawyer tried again to visit, only to have the door shut to him again. Then, the next night, he went to Dr. Lanyon's.

There, at least, he was welcomed. However, when he went inside, he was shocked at the change in his friend's appearance. Dr. Lanyon had the ghostly look of a man who is about to die, or who fears that death is about to strike him.

"What has happened to you, Lanyon?" asked the lawyer in dismay.

"I am a doomed man," replied Lanyon. "Life has been pleasant. I have liked it well enough. But now I have entered a state of shock from which I will never recover. I am only glad that I have avoided this kind of torture for this long. Now, I am ready to surrender to it."

"Lanyon! Get a grip, my good man!" exclaimed Utterson. "Jekyll is ill, too. Have you seen him? I haven't been able to make it past the front door."

Then Lanyon's eyes turned dark and he shuddered. "I wish to see or hear no more of Dr. Jekyll," he said in a hoarse voice. "I am finished with that person. He is dead to me."

Utterson opened his mouth, but no words came out. He didn't know what to say or do next.

Lanyon put an end to the silence. "After I am dead," he said, "I hope that you find out the truth. If you wish to stay and discuss another matter, please do. If not, please go, for I cannot bear it."

When Utterson got home, he wrote the following letter to Dr. Jekyll:

My dear and honorable friend,
Why do I arrive at your door only to have it shut in my face? How did I, of all people, suddenly become

unworthy of your friendship? Not to
mention the good Dr. Lanyon. We
were probably the best friends you
will ever have in your lifetime. Can't
our "cheese sandwich" remain
whole, as we planned? Must each
separate piece become food for lab
rats in the end? Only the three of us
know what that means. Surely this
must tell you something! I hope for
a speedy, honest reply and the
chance to remain—
    Truly yours—the cheese between
two pieces of bread,
                Gabriel John Utterson, Esq.

The next day brought a long and
unusually serious reply:

Dear solitary cheese,
    I fear that it is too late for us to go
back to being a "sandwich." We may
be just food for the rats now. I can't
tell you how sorry I am. I share

Lanyon's view that we must never meet again. I wish to lead the rest of my life alone, as a plain "slice of bread." My layers have been stripped, and I cannot bear to be seen. I have sinned and now I suffer in the darkest way. I am sure that I deserve this, but my dear old friends do not. Utterson, I wish I could tell you more, but it is better to remain silent. Please respect that. I now remain—

Truly alone,
Dr. Henry E. Jekyll

Utterson was amazed beyond belief. These great changes in both Jekyll and

Lanyon were somehow connected. But how? The lawyer was unsure whether he would ever know.

Two weeks later, Dr. Lanyon died in his sleep. The night after his funeral, Utterson went into his study and locked the door. Sitting by the light of a lone candle, he took an envelope out of his coat pocket. Written on the front were these words: *"PRIVATE. For the hands of G. J. Utterson alone. If he dies before opening this, it is to be destroyed unread."* The handwriting was that of the dead doctor.

Taking a deep breath, the lawyer

opened the envelope, only to find another envelope. This one was marked as follows: *"Not to be opened until the death or disappearance of Dr. Henry Jekyll."* Utterson could not believe his eyes.

Pacing back and forth between his desk and the safe, he wanted to rip the envelope open. But professional honor and faith in his dead friend stopped him. The envelope stayed sealed in a corner of his private safe.

Over the next few days, Utterson's restlessness and curiosity kept growing. Time and again, the lawyer found himself at Jekyll's doorstep. He felt more satisfied with the daily reports from Poole than if he had been shown into the house.

Poole, however, did not have very pleasant news for the unwanted guest. Dr. Jekyll now kept himself in the office over his laboratory. He never asked for anyone's company or even read a book.

Chapter 8

A REMARKABLE
CHANGE

*I*t just so happened that on one of the usual Sunday walks taken by Mr. Utterson and his cousin, Mr. Enfield, they somehow ended up on the same street where each had first seen Edward Hyde.

"Thank goodness Hyde is gone forever!" said Enfield.

"I hope you are right," said Utterson. "I am worried about Jekyll. Let's step into the courtyard. Even if we can't go inside the lab, perhaps we can get his attention through the office window. Maybe we can visit with him that way."

"I didn't know that this was so close to Jekyll's home!" exclaimed Enfield as they entered the courtyard.

"Yes, indeed. I found it out only recently myself," said Utterson just as the sun began to set. "Oh, look, there he is!"

There, sitting beside a half-open window, was Dr. Jekyll. He stared out with a blank look, like a man stuck in a prison cell. Then his eye caught Utterson's and he quickly began to shut the window.

"What? Hey, Jekyll!" the lawyer called out. "Wait! How are you feeling?"

Jekyll hesitated, then opened the window again. He held out his hand to keep the two men from coming any closer. They had to squint their eyes to see him better. He looked pale and—well, different somehow.

"I am not well, Utterson," said Jekyll. "It will not last long, though, thank goodness."

"You stay indoors too much," said Utterson. "This is my cousin, Mr.

Richard Enfield. Would you care to join us for some fresh air?"

"Thank you for thinking of me. However, I cannot. I dare not!"

"Very well then, old friend," said Utterson. "We'll just stay put and talk to you from right here."

"I would like that very much," said the doctor. But when the two men began to come closer, Jekyll slammed the window shut and disappeared.

Not until Utterson and Enfield reached the busy center of town did they say a single word to one another. When Utterson finally turned to look at his companion, he saw the same horror in his cousin's eyes that he himself felt.

"We should never have gone there," said Utterson. Mr. Enfield only nodded his head in agreement. They walked on in silence once more.

Chapter 9

A CHILLING
DISCOVERY

One evening after dinner, Mr. Utterson was quite surprised to receive a visit from Poole. From the worried look on the butler's face, the lawyer gathered that he had much on his mind.

"What brings you here, Poole?" the lawyer asked. "What worries you so?"

"You know how the doctor shuts himself up in that cramped office, sir. Well, he is shut up in there again. I just don't like the looks of things, sir, and—"

"Yes, Poole, what is it?" asked Utterson, growing impatient.

"It's just that I'm afraid, sir, and I can bear it no longer," Poole replied, without saying exactly what frightened him.

"Please," begged the lawyer. "Just relax, Poole. I can see that something is upsetting you, and it must be very serious. Please, just tell me what it is."

"Well, sir, you see—" he paused, then said quickly, "I think that there has been foul play."

"Foul play!" exclaimed the lawyer. "What are you saying?"

"I dare not say, sir," said Poole. Seeing the lawyer so upset made the butler feel even worse. "Why don't you come with me and see for yourself?"

It was a cold, windy March night. Overhead, wispy clouds flew by in a fury, as if they were whipping up a great storm. Mr. Utterson pulled his coat snugly around his shivering body. He followed Poole, who kept a step or two ahead. The streets they crossed were totally empty.

After what seemed like ages, they reached Dr. Jekyll's front door. Poole knocked with three short knocks.

"Is that you, Poole?" a whispering voice asked from within.

"Yes, it's all right. Let us in," said Poole. They entered to find all of Dr. Jekyll's servants huddled around the fireplace in the hallway.

"What is going on here?" asked the lawyer.

"They are all afraid," said Poole.

"Of what?"

"Please, follow me, sir," said Poole. He led the way by the light of a lamp, the flame of which flickered in the icy wind.

Utterson shivered and suddenly felt that he should run the other way. But his feet continued to follow Poole. Finally, the two men arrived at the door to the doctor's office. As Poole turned to face Utterson, the light from the lamp cast a spooky glow on the butler's pale face.

"Now, sir," he said, "if for some reason the doctor asks you in, don't go."

Utterson's nerves were on edge. The muscles in his legs twitched. He would have lost his balance if Poole hadn't grabbed his arm at just the right moment.

"Please, sir, whatever you do, just try to stay calm," said Poole. He took a deep breath, then knocked on the door. He motioned for the lawyer to press his ear against it.

"Mr. Utterson is here, sir, asking to see you," Poole called out.

A voice answered from within, "Tell him I cannot see anyone."

Poole said nothing. Taking up his lamp, he led Mr. Utterson back across the yard and into the doctor's kitchen.

"Sir," he said, "you have now heard it as well as I. That is not the doctor's voice! It has been replaced by a low, gritty-sounding one."

Feeling faint, Utterson quickly took a nearby seat. "Well, perhaps poor Jekyll is very ill. Maybe that made his voice take on a new tone."

"No, sir. I have lived here for twenty years. I know his voice well. I'm afraid that someone has done away with the doctor! Eight days ago, the other servants and I heard him cry out in sheer terror. Whoever killed the good doctor is now locked in that office!"

"That sounds like a rather wild explanation, Poole," said Utterson. "If it were true, why would the murderer stay? It just doesn't make sense."

"I believe I can prove it to you," replied Poole. "For the past eight days, whoever—or whatever—lives in that office has been crying, night and day. He is begging for some sort of medicine.

When the doctor ordered drugs for a patient, he would write what he needed on a slip of paper. He would leave that on the stairs for me, and I would go get it. Well, this week there have been two or three slips of paper each day, asking for the same drug. Every time I bring it back, there is another note telling me to take it back, because it is not pure. Someone wants that drug very badly, sir. I wish I knew what it was for."

"Do you have any of these slips of paper?" asked Mr. Utterson

Poole took a crumpled note out of his pocket and handed it to the lawyer.

"Sirs," the lawyer read, "Dr. Jekyll has found your last sample to be impure. In the year 18—, you sold Dr. Jekyll some that was pure. If any of the same is left, please send it to him at once. For heaven's sake, find some of the old brew!"

"This is a strange note," said Utterson. "All at once, at the very end, comes an outburst of emotion. Why do you still have this note if you were supposed to take it to the drugstore?"

"The man at the shop was very angry and insulted, sir. He threw it back at me," replied Poole.

"I still don't understand why you think the doctor has been murdered. This looks like his handwriting."

"What does it matter if it looks like the doctor's handwriting?" said Poole, upset. "I have seen the creature who stays in Dr. Jekyll's office!"

"You have seen him? Well, go on my good man!" exclaimed Utterson. He began to pace nervously back and forth.

"It happened this way," Poole told him. "I had come into the laboratory for my nightly call. The creature must have come out of the office to look for this drug. There he was at the far end of the room, digging among the boxes. When he saw me, he yelled like a wounded animal. Then he dashed up-stairs to the office. I saw him for only a moment, but my hair stood on end and goose bumps covered my skin. I know that it wasn't the doctor wearing a mask, because this creature was so short. The good doctor was a tall man with a fine build. I believe in my heart that a murder was committed!"

"We both know who this man is, don't we, Poole?" Utterson said.

"Yes, sir. I saw him very quickly, but

I think it was Mr. Hyde. I could tell by the chill I felt in my bones. Who else could have gotten in by the laboratory door?"

"Indeed! I believe you," said Mr. Utterson. "I believe that poor Jekyll has been killed, and that the murderer still lurks in his office. But why? For now, I think it is my duty to break in that door."

"Ah! Very well, then!" said Poole with much relief. "I will help you." He went to

get an ax, then asked two other servants to stand guard at the laboratory door.

When the lawyer and the butler arrived once more at the office door, they could hear footsteps inside. These steps fell slowly and lightly, different from the doctor's quick, heavy steps.

"Is there ever any other noise?" whispered Mr. Utterson.

"Once I heard it weeping like a lost soul. I could have wept myself, after hearing that," answered Poole.

Utterson gathered up his courage, then called out in a loud voice, "Jekyll! I demand to see you." No reply. "If you don't let me in, I will be forced to break down this door! Your unusual habits have made us suspicious."

"Utterson," said the gritty voice. "Please, have mercy!"

"That is not the voice of Dr. Jekyll. It is Mr. Hyde's!" shouted Utterson. "Down with the door, Poole!"

The butler swung the ax at the

wooden door with all his might. The building shook, but the door stayed solid. A scream rang out from the office. The ax struck again, but the wood was strong. Not until the fifth blow did the door fly open.

Stunned by the sudden stillness, Utterson and Poole stood back and peered inside. A fire burned in the fireplace, heating a kettle. Papers sat neatly on the desk. A teapot and cup sat on the table.

In the middle of the room lay a twitching body. Drawing on his courage, Utterson rolled the body over. He was staring at Hyde's face.

Cold beads of sweat formed on the lawyer's forehead as he felt for a heartbeat. There was none. The wicked Edward Hyde was dead.

"He is holding an empty tube in his hand," said Utterson. "He must have

swallowed a dangerous chemical. We have come too late to save him or to punish him. Now all that is left for us is to find the body of Dr. Jekyll."

"He must be buried somewhere in this building," said Poole. The two men searched the laboratory, but found no trace of Henry Jekyll, dead or alive.

"Let's go back to the office and check there again," said the lawyer.

They climbed the stairs in silence. Once again, they searched every inch of the office. On one table were traces of a chemical experiment—small piles of a white powder laid out on glass dishes.

"That is the same drug I had been bringing him," said Poole. Just then, the kettle began to boil, giving off a startling whistle. This drew the men over near the desk, where they saw a large envelope on top of all the papers. It was addressed to Mr. Utterson, written in the doctor's hand. The lawyer opened it and took out a will like the one in his safe at home. All of the terms were the same, but for one: In place of Edward Hyde's name as inheritor was the name Gabriel John Utterson!

"I am shocked!" he said. "Hyde had this will all this time.Why didn't he destroy it? He must have been outraged to find himself betrayed by the doctor. I just don't understand."

He noticed a letter with the will. It was written in the doctor's hand, with that day's date at the top. "Oh, Poole!" the lawyer cried, "Jekyll was alive and here *today!* He could not have been killed and gotten rid of in such a short time. He must have fled! But how? To where?"

"Why don't you read the note, sir?" asked Poole.

My dear Utterson,
When you read this, I shall have disappeared, although how or why, I have no idea. But I feel sure that the end is near. Please read Lanyon's report, which he warned me he would give to you. Then, if you care to learn more, read my confession.
Your unworthy, unhappy friend,
Henry Jekyll

"Is there more?" asked Utterson.

"Yes. Here is another envelope addressed to you, sir," said Poole. He picked up a heavy packet and handed it to the lawyer.

Utterson put it in his coat pocket. "Say nothing to anyone about this, Poole," he then said. "Whatever has become of the doctor, we must protect his good name. I'm off for home to read these papers in quiet. I shall be back before midnight. Then, and only then, we shall call for the police."

They left the building, locking the door of the laboratory behind them. Utterson walked back to his house.

Now that he was about to learn the answers to so many dreadful questions, the lawyer suddenly realized that he was afraid to find out the truth. Still, in many ways, he was eager to clear up this mystery, once and for all.

Chapter 10

DR. LANYON'S REPORT

*H*eaving a great sigh, Mr. Utterson sat in his chair near the fire and enjoyed the quiet. He decided to take a minute to calm his nerves and collect his thoughts. Only then would he study the papers that could change his life forever.

Suddenly, there was a strange flicker from the fireplace and he saw shadows move across the wall. Utterson glanced quickly over his shoulder but saw no one. Then he heard a slow, sad whistle that jerked him right out of his chair.

"Oh, I'm afraid my nerves are completely shot! The wind is simply whistling its way through the open window. I must go and shut it before I give in to my ridiculous fright."

After he shut the window, he thought he heard a soft, cackling laughter. Where was it coming from? The chimney! He stepped over to the fireplace, but all he heard were logs crackling as they burned.

"No more of this nonsense!" thought the lawyer. "I must keep my head if I'm going to get through these papers

tonight." He sat down, took out Dr. Lanyon's report, and read:

Four days ago, I received a letter addressed to me in the handwriting of my old school friend Henry Jekyll. I was very surprised because I had dined with him just the night before.

His letter said that he needed my help with a very important matter. He went on to say that his life, honor, and sanity were all at my mercy. He swore that if I failed him, he would be lost. He asked me to put off all my other plans for that night. He instructed me to drive to his house, where Poole had been given orders to let me in. Then, I was to enter his office—by force, if necessary. I was to take some things from a particular drawer and take them back to my home. The drawer would contain some powders, a glass jar, and a notebook.

Furthermore, I was told to make sure that I was back at my house well before midnight. When the clock struck twelve, a stranger would arrive at my doorstep. I was to let him in and give him the things that had been in the drawer. This was all I had to do to win the good doctor's favor.

I received no explanations, just a tug at my heart strings. "If you fail to do any of these things I ask," Jekyll had written, "you may charge your conscience with my death or madness."

You can see why I felt I must do as he asked. I understood so little of this mess. I was in no position to judge what was important and what was not. I took my old friend's word and set out to do what he asked.

Wasting no time, I hopped into a cab and drove straight to Jekyll's house. I was greeted by Poole, who had been given instructions similar to mine. He had already sent for a locksmith and a carpenter. They had been working for almost an hour by then, trying to open the locked office door without causing much damage. Finally, after another hour, the locksmith succeeded.

My eyes darted around the room, stopping every now and then to notice a broken bottle or pages torn from a book. Nothing I saw explained the bizarre situation. I left with the drawer, its contents, and more questions than I arrived with.

When I returned home, I studied

the items closely. The powders were in unmarked containers. It was clear that they had been mixed by Jekyll, not given to him that way. The glass jar was about half full of a blood-red liquid that had a strong, bitter smell. I didn't know what it was. The notebook contained nothing but a list of dates. This covered a period of many years, but the last date in the list was nearly a year ago. The only other note in the book was written next to a date very early in the list. It said, "TOTAL FAILURE!!!" It looked to me as if Jekyll had been keeping a record of a series of experiments.

I could not understand how my having these things would affect my friend's honor, sanity, or life. I began to think that the poor doctor had come down with a disease of the brain. Perhaps he was dangerous. I wondered if I would need some kind of self-defense when this stranger arrived, so I loaded an old gun.

The clock had barely struck midnight when I heard a soft knock at the door. The noise startled me, but I went to the door at once.

Before opening it, I asked, "Are you the man sent here by Dr. Jekyll?"

"Yes, yes," the man whispered urgently. He asked me to let him in. When I opened the door, he quickly entered and shut the door behind him.

As I followed him into the brightly lit den I kept my hand on my gun— just in case. There, I finally had the chance to see him clearly. Once I did, though, I wanted to dim the lights. He was small but muscular, and had a nasty look on his face. I hated him, but could not have given any reason why.

This creature was dressed in a laughable fashion. His clothes were expensive and well-made, but were enormous on him. The legs of his pants were rolled up to keep them from dragging on the ground, and his collar spread wide upon his shoulders. But I certainly didn't laugh.

In fact, I was horrified. His ill-fitting clothes simply made his freakish qualities worse. They also made me even more curious to know who he was, how he lived, and where on earth he came from.

"Have you got the stuff?" he cried. He was so impatient that he grabbed my arm and began to shake me.

I pried his fingers off me, feeling an icy pang in my blood at his touch. I

showed him to a comfortable seat and sat down in my own chair. It took great effort for me to appear at ease, due to my fears and the horror I felt toward my visitor. But I did the best I could.

"Come, sir," I said. "You forget that I have not yet had a chance to get to know you."

"I beg your pardon," he replied in a strained but polite manner. "My impatience has overcome my politeness. I apologize, but I—" He paused and put his hand on his throat. I could see, in spite of his collected manner, that he was trying to hold back a hysterical outburst. "The drawer!" he growled. "Please, sir, if you will."

I took pity on my visitor. Perhaps I also was giving in to my growing curiosity. "There it is, sir," I said, pointing to the drawer on the floor, still covered with a sheet.

The animal sprung to it. I could hear him grunting and his teeth grating. His eyes bulged out of his head and he began to foam at the mouth! I grew alarmed both for his life and his sanity.

"Pull yourself together!" I said as he pulled off the sheet.

At the sight of the contents, he gave a loud sob of relief. "Do you have a measuring cup?" he asked, trying to maintain self-control.

I rose from my seat nervously and gave him what he asked for.

He nodded in thanks and measured out some of the red liquid, then added one of the powders. At first, the mixture was a reddish color, but as the crystals melted, it began to brighten in color. It bubbled and threw off steam. Suddenly, the bubbling stopped and the mixture turned a dark purple, which then faded to a watery green. My visitor watched these changes with a sharp eye. He then smiled, set the cup down on the table, and turned to me.

"Now, will you be satisfied if I leave with this cup in hand, or has your curiosity gotten too powerful? Think before you answer," he warned,

"for I shall do as you decide. If you choose to witness what comes next, you will behold scientific knowledge like none you had thought existed. Here, in this room, new avenues to fame and power will be as open to you as they have been for me."

"Sir," I said, trying to appear calm, "I don't know what you speak of. But I have gone along too far already—without any explanations. I will not miss the chance to see the end."

"So you shall," replied the visitor. "Lanyon, remember your promise! What follows is strictly confidential. You can tell no one! You have always stuck to the most narrow views of science. You have always denied the endless possibilities of medicine. You have always looked down on some of your fellow scientists. Now you—you, Hastie Lanyon—behold!"

He put the cup to his lips and drank the liquid in one gulp. An animal

cry followed. He staggered backward and clutched the table to keep from falling. Staring straight at me with a gasping mouth, his face suddenly turned black. His features seemed to melt and rearrange. His body seemed to swell. I could not watch any longer. I lifted my arm to shield my eyes.

Suddenly, the noises stopped and there was silence. I peered out from behind my arm and almost fainted at what I saw before me. There before my eyes, pale and shaking like a man back from death, stood Henry Jekyll!

What he told me in the next hour, I cannot bear to write down.

I saw what I saw, I heard what I heard. Yet now I ask myself if I believe it. I cannot answer. My soul is sick with shock and grief. I don't know what is real and what is not—my sanity has left me. I feel that my days are numbered.

I must tell you one more thing, Utterson, if you can bring yourself to believe it. The creature who crept into my house that night was, by Jekyll's own confession, known by the name of Edward Hyde.

And now I bid you good-bye.
Hastie Lanyon

Chapter
11

A SHOCKING
CONFESSION

*T*aking a deep breath, Utterson looked at the fireplace, where a lively fire burned. Just as he was about to read Henry Jekyll's confession, he thought he saw two faces staring back at him from the flames. He rose from his chair and went to the fireplace. Oddly, he felt no fear. When he bent down to get a closer look, a voice surrounded him, as if it were coming from everywhere. In the fire, he saw the faces of Dr. Jekyll and Mr. Hyde.

"Don't be frightened," the voice said. "We are one, Mr. Hyde and I. I am his good, while he is my evil."

It was Jekyll's voice! Or was it Hyde's? "What is that supposed to mean?" the lawyer asked the flickering flames.

"It means that both good and evil live in all of us," said the voice. "One cannot exist without the other. I found a way to bring out my evil side. I thought I could do so without harming my good side. That, I have learned, is not possible.

"But the valuable lesson I wish to pass on to you, dear friend, is this: Do not try to adjust your true nature. The balance that must be struck between good and evil is born within you. That was my mistake—not knowing this. I thought that I had the power to put one above the other whenever I wished. Now I know that I was wrong."

Then the two faces faded from the fire, and Utterson was left staring into ordinary orange flames. After a while, he went back to his chair, sat down, and slowly opened Henry Jekyll's confession.

I was born in the year 18— to a large fortune. My family taught me to respect the wise and the good among my fellow human beings. The worst of my faults was a careless spirit of the heart. In its way, it has made many people happy, but it also has caused me much trouble. As a scientist, I wished to be taken seriously by other scientists and experts.

I began to hide my youthful activities, because I worried that some people would think me childish and irresponsible. Another man may have bragged about being playful and fun-loving. But I set high standards for myself, so I judged myself harshly. It was those strict standards that made

me feel guilty and shameful of my behavior.

It was this sense of self-doubt that split my one nature into two separate parts, good and bad. I began leading a double life. I was as much myself when I was doing shameful deeds as I was when I worked hard to relieve people's sorrow and suffering.

It is not surprising that my scientific studies eventually led me to discover the truth—that a person is not truly one, but two. It is that knowledge that can make all the difference.

Even before my studies on the two-sided nature of people began, I used to daydream. I dreamed about being able to separate good from evil. After all, in any one person, there is a constant struggle between these two forces. If the two could be placed in separate bodies, each would be able to thrive without being threatened by the other one. That is what I told myself, anyway.

As I started thinking about it more and more, I began to experiment. I mixed drugs day and night, looking for something with the power to change a person's identity. It was the ultimate challenge! Finally, I found the last ingredient and bought a lot of it.

Late one fateful night, I mixed the chemicals and watched them boil and

smoke in the glass. Then, with a healthy dose of courage, I drank the potion.

All at once, my body trembled and I felt an agony like never before. Then suddenly I felt like myself again, as if coming out of a terrible illness. But there was something strange and new. I felt younger, lighter, and healthier. I felt reckless and irresponsible. At once, I knew that I had turned wicked.

Instantly, I became aware that I had shrunk in height. But there was no mirror in my office. I had to see myself! I decided to sneak to my bedroom. At that late hour, no one would notice— everyone would be asleep. As I crossed the yard, I thought with wonder that I must be the first creature of this sort ever seen by the stars. It gave me a thrill. I quietly walked through the hall-ways to my room. There, I saw Edward Hyde for the first time.

I don't know for sure, but I suppose that, at that time, the evil side of my nature was weaker than the good. After all, up till then I had led a life of mostly good deeds and self-control. The evil side had been much less active.

I believe that is why Edward Hyde was so much smaller, thinner, and younger than Henry Jekyll. But evil had made Hyde's face and body seem ugly and deformed. Yet, when I looked into the mirror, I saw a welcome sight, not a disgusting one. After all, this creature, too, was myself. To me, it seemed natural and human.

When I was Hyde, no one could come near me without showing some obvious sign of discomfort. This most likely was because Hyde was pure evil. Others did not wish to see this because, if they did, they might see the evil in themselves.

I lingered only a moment at the mirror, for I had work to do. I needed to perform a second experiment to see if I could become Henry Jekyll again. If not, I had to run from this house—it would be mine no longer.

Hurrying back to my office, I pre-pared and drank the potion. I suffered the same agony of change. This time, I became myself again. I had the height, personality, and face of Dr. Jekyll.

It was done! I had succeeded in sep-arating good and evil. But wait! Jekyll was not all good, the way Hyde was all evil. Jekyll suffered from the struggle of the two forces. Both still remained in me. Instead of creating separate homes for good and evil, I had unleashed a monster without setting free an angel.

Even knowing this and feeling guilty for what I had done, I had not yet learned my lesson. Tempted by my new powers, I wanted to drink the potion over and over. During this time, I rented a house in Soho for Mr. Hyde.

As Jekyll, I told my servants that a Mr. Hyde was to be allowed to freely roam my house. Several times in the weeks that followed, I made sure to visit the house as Hyde. Next, I drew up that will you were so suspicious of. I did it so that if anything happened to Jekyll, I could still keep my property as Hyde.

Finally, I felt ready to lead my double life. Many people hire others to do their dirty work. Using my alter ego, I could perform wicked deeds without anyone recognizing me. It *was* me, but it *wasn't* me! One moment, I could be standing tall with a wave of respect washing over me. The next, I could dive headfirst into a sea of recklessness. Best of all, Dr. Henry Jekyll's good name would remain unharmed.

When I first decided to have fun as my other self, the things I wanted to do may have been foolish, but not harmful. In the hands of Mr. Hyde, however, they began to turn monstrous. When I became Dr. Jekyll again after my evil outings, I was full of horror and regret.

Still, I was at the mercy of the monster. His every act and thought centered on himself. In time, Henry Jekyll was able to soothe his conscience somewhat. After all, it was not *he* who was guilty of these sins. By trying to undo the evils done by Hyde, Jekyll was able to put his mind even more at ease.

I am sure that you are wondering just what types of wickedness Hyde took part in. However, I can think of no good reason to tell you much more than you already know. Why should I let you

think any worse of me than you already must?

Believe it or not, I am still the same man who is the friend you know so well. In fact, you probably know more about me than you care to admit to yourself— even things that I dare not write down here. For you, Gabriel John Utterson, know me better than anyone else. So perhaps you are not as shocked as you may feel. Think about it. Look inside yourself, and surely you shall see the truth. Therefore, I will spare you the details. Read on! I have more to tell you about the events that led to my final transformation.

Utterson paused, rubbed his eyes, and gazed briefly into the fire. Then, hungry to learn more, he turned the page and read on.

Chapter 12

THE LESSER OF
TWO EVILS

About two months before the murder of Sir Danvers Carew, I had been out for one of Hyde's adventures and returned at a late hour. Immediately, I swallowed the potion and went to sleep as Henry Jekyll. The next day, though, I woke with an odd feeling.

Looking around, I could see the fancy furniture and high ceilings of my room. However, something felt wrong, as if I were not actually where I seemed to be. I was in Dr. Jekyll's room, but felt as if I were in the little room in Soho where I sometimes slept as Hyde.

Still waking from a dream state, I kept my eyes closed. Lazily, I began to question my confusion. I realized that I was beginning to have trouble remembering who I had been last. This thought made me chuckle. How silly of me! Of course I was Jekyll! I had gone to sleep as Henry Jekyll. I was in my house in the grand square. Then I opened my eyes and looked at my hand.

Utterson, you know the hand of Henry Jekyll as well as I do. It is large and firm, with well-manicured fingernails. Well, the hand that I saw lying on the bedspread at that moment was small, full of veins, and had jagged yellow fingernails. Needless to say, I was suddenly wide awake, sitting upright. It was the hand of Edward Hyde!

I must have stared at it for five minutes. I was numb, in a daze. I felt as if drums were banging in my head. Finally, I rushed to the mirror. At

the sight of Hyde, my blood went icy and I trembled from head to toe.

Yes, I had gone to bed as Henry Jekyll and awakened as Edward Hyde, without a drop of the potion!

How was this to be explained? How was it to be fixed? It was about ten o'clock in the morning, so all of the servants were up and about. All of my drugs were in the office—a long journey down two sets of stairs, through the back passage, across the courtyard, and through the laboratory! Even if I covered my face, how would that help when I couldn't hide my smaller size?

Before I began to panic, relief poured over me. I realized that the servants were already used to visits by my second self. I quickly dressed in clothes of my own size. As soon as I opened the bedroom door and dashed out, I crashed into Randi, the maid, in the hall. She stared and gasped at seeing Mr. Hyde at such an odd hour of

the day—and coming out of the doctor's room! I ran past her and managed to avoid the others. Ten minutes later, Dr. Jekyll returned and sat down to breakfast in the kitchen.

Small indeed was my appetite, yet I forced myself to sip some tea and eat half a muffin—out of the four sitting on my dish. The cook was used to watching me eat large shares of his homemade treats

every morning. He knew that something was not quite right. When he noticed my sweaty brow, he brought me a cold, damp towel and asked if I was ill. "Thank you, Eric," I managed to say, then excused myself and went to my office.

Here I sat and began to reflect, more seriously than ever before, on the problems of my double life. It seemed as though Edward Hyde's body had grown

lately. Perhaps it was because his personality was growing stronger. He was taking
over! Jekyll was slowly losing the voluntary power to make Hyde come and go.

I thought back to my early work.
Once, very early in my experiments, the
drug had totally failed me. Several times
since then, I had doubled or even
tripled the dose! At that time, it was

because I was having trouble changing from doctor to devil. Now, it seemed, I would need greater doses to do the opposite. It was clear that my original and better self was slipping away.

Between Jekyll and Hyde, I felt that I now had to choose. I was sure that if I did not take the matter into my hands while I still could, Hyde would not give me the chance.

I thought about what each had to offer. They had the same memories, but everything else was unevenly shared between them. The doctor, kind and decent in many ways, still shared in the pleasures and adventures of his evil other self. After all, Jekyll was the one who had come up with plans for Hyde to act upon. But Hyde didn't care about his creator. He thought of Jekyll only the way an outlaw thinks of the hideout that keeps him from getting caught.

To give up Hyde and live as Jekyll would be to lay my devilish appetite to rest. I would surely suffer without it. But to destroy Jekyll and live as Hyde would be to kill a thousand hopes and dreams, and to become forever hated and friendless. There was something else to think about: While Jekyll would suffer greatly for what he had lost, Hyde would not care a bit about losing his better half.

After tossing the choices back and forth in my mind, I chose my better side and prayed for the strength to keep to it. It's true! I preferred to be the doctor, a regular man surrounded by friends and holding dear his honest hopes. I said good-bye to the liberty, the youth and energy, and the secret pleasure—a final farewell to Edward Hyde. Still, I didn't give up the house in Soho, nor did I destroy Hyde's clothes. I can't explain why.

For two months, I held myself to strict standards like never before. But it didn't last long. I began to grow impatient, as if Hyde were struggling for freedom. At last, in an hour of weakness, I once again mixed and swallowed the dreadful potion.

I was unprepared for what followed. I didn't realize that, in effect, I had caged an animal and was now letting him loose. The moment I drank the potion, I felt a storm brewing in my soul—and Hyde came out roaring! He was furious and wild, with a wicked hunger much greater than before.

Soon after making my transformation, I met Sir Danvers Carew, who was unfortunate enough to cross my path. As I heard him ask me politely for directions, I became impatient and angry, for no good reason. It certainly wasn't that poor man's fault.

With a hysterical outburst, I hit the man with my cane. As I committed this unforgivable crime, I felt a cold rush of terror flowing through my veins. A light flickered somewhere inside me, and suddenly I understood what I had just done. Quickly, I fled from the scene.

I ran to the house in Soho and destroyed my papers, which were proof of my double life. Then I set out through the streets, bragging about my crime, yet still trembling at the idea that it had been done. Hyde had a song upon his lips as he mixed and drank the potion.

With tears of thankfulness and remorse, I fell on my knees as Henry Jekyll. My mind was flooded with horrible images from my twisted memory. But I continued to cry and pray.

As the remorse faded, it was followed by a feeling of joy. After all, now I was inside the body and mind of Dr. Jekyll. Hyde didn't have to be brought back. Oh, how I rejoiced to think that! I was so happy to be normal again! With determination, I left my office, locked its door, and smashed the key under my heel.

The next day, I heard the news of the murder cried out in the square.

"Hyde is the culprit!" people said. Jekyll
was my safety net. If Hyde peeped out for
even an instant, the men of London
would be out to capture him.

For my past sins, I promised to be a better person. I can say with honesty that my promises were truthful. I cannot say that I got tired of this unselfish and innocent life. I think I enjoyed it more than ever. As I fulfilled my promises, though, I began to feel less and less regretful. Soon the darker side of me growled for attention again. Not that I even dreamed of bringing Hyde back to life!

In the end, however, it was in the mind and body of Henry Jekyll that I was once more tempted to dabble in bad deeds. So I did.

It was this brief failure that finally destroyed me. Yet somehow, I was not alarmed. It seemed natural—like a return to the old days before I had made my discovery.

Chapter 13

THE FINAL
TRANSFORMATION

*I*t was a fine, clear January day, with frost melting on the ground and clear skies overhead. Regent's Park was full of birds and spring smells. I sat in the sun on a bench, the animal within me calm and satisfied for the moment. The angel in me promised to make up for it, but was not yet moved to begin.

I smiled as I compared myself to others—my active goodwill to their lazy carelessness. At that very moment, I felt horribly sick to my stomach and began to shiver. These waves of illness passed and left me feeling faint. All at once, I was aware of a change in my mood and my thoughts.

Suddenly, I felt a greater boldness and less fear of danger, I looked down. My clothes hung on my shrunken limbs. The hand that lay on my knee was small and hairy. Without even drinking the potion, I was Edward Hyde once more! A moment before I had been safe, respected, and admired. Now I was hunted, home-less, and hated.

My sanity wavered, but it did not fail me completely. In my second self, my senses seemed sharpened to a point. Therefore, in situations where Jekyll may have failed, Hyde rose to the importance of the moment. How was I to reach my drugs? They were in a drawer in my office. That was the problem Hyde set out to solve. I struggled to think.

I had shut and locked the laboratory door for good. There was no longer a key. If I tried to enter by the house, my own servants would call the police and have me captured. I realized that I would need help. I thought of Lanyon. How could I convince him to help me? How could I even get to his house? Then I remembered that I could write in the good doctor's handwriting! Once I had that spark of hope, the rest of the plan lit up on its own.

Catching a passing cab, I drove to a hotel on Portland Street. At my appear-

ance, which was indeed funny, the cab driver could not hide his laughter. I kept my self-control until we reached the hotel. Then I whacked him with my new cane. The smile fled from his face.

As I entered the hotel I snarled at the staff, who kept their eyes away from me. They took my orders and led me to a private room. Here I would write to Dr. Lanyon and beg for his help.

Hyde, now in danger, was a new creature to me. He was shaken with great anger, his nerves high-strung. Yet the creature was clever and controlled himself. He wrote two important letters—one to Dr. Lanyon and one to Poole—and sent them out.

From that point on, Hyde sat all day near the fire in his private room. There he dined, sitting alone with his fears. Then, when the sky had turned completely black, he took a cab to Lanyon's house. Nothing lived in Hyde but fear and hatred. When at last the driver dropped him on the corner of Lanyon's street, these two emotions raged within him. He walked fast, haunted by his fears and chattering to himself. He was counting the minutes until midnight—still half an hour away.

When I came back to myself at Lanyon's, I realized that another change had come over me. It was no longer the fear of being caught for murder that upset me—it was the horror of being Hyde. I barely remember what I said to Lanyon or what he said to me. It was partly in a dream that I went home to my own house and got into bed. I fell into a deep sleep that even the terrible nightmares couldn't break. I awoke in the morning shaken and weak, but refreshed. I still hated and feared the thought of the brute who slept within me, but I felt safe in the comfort of home, close to my drugs.

After breakfast, I was strolling leiserely across the courtyard when I was seized again with those painful feelings of change. I raced to my office, but could not stop Hyde from coming out before I got there. It took a double dose

of the potion to bring me back to myself this time. But just six short hours later, the pains returned and I had to take the drug once more.

From that day forth, I was able to stay as Jekyll only by constantly taking the drug. At all hours of the day or night, I would feel the attacks of the transformation. Above all, if I slept or even dozed a moment in my chair, I always awoke as Hyde. Under the steady strain of this doom, I became ill. Fevers burned me up and my mind had only one thought—the horror of my other self. When I slept or the medicine wore off, I would leap into images of terror. My body seemed too weak to contain the force of that other life. Hyde's powers seemed to grow with the illness of Jekyll.

Certainly, the hate that split them was not equal on each side. Hyde's hatred for Jekyll was intense. His terror of being captured drove him to return to the body of Jekyll, but he hated needing to do so. Hyde hated the good doctor for turning against him. As punishment, he burned my letters, scribbled on the pages of my books, and destroyed the painting of my father.

Jekyll hated Hyde because he had seen the full deformity of the creature that shared some of his mind. He saw Hyde as lifeless. It was shocking to Jekyll that this creature had a voice and could make gestures. It was even more horrifying that this heartless beast was closer to him than a wife. Jekyll kept feeling Hyde's struggle to be born at the cost of his creator's life. Somehow, though, when I think about how Hyde feared my power to cut him off by killing myself, I found it in my heart to pity him.

Now that my tale has been told, it is useless to go on about my suffering. No one has ever suffered such agony. Let that be enough. My punishment might

have gone on for years, if not for the last disaster to happen. My supply of the drug, which had not been renewed since the first experiment, began to run low. I sent for more and mixed the potion. The bubbling followed and so did the first change of color, but not the second. I drank it anyway, but nothing happened. Frightened at what would become of me, I asked Poole to search all of London for some as pure as the original. It came to nothing. I now realize that my first supply must have been *im*pure, not pure. It was the unknown impurity that allowed me to succeed in the first place.

About a week has gone by. I am now finishing this statement after taking the last of the old powders. I write this as Henry Jekyll, respected doctor and friend. This is the last time that Jekyll will be able to think his own thoughts or see his own face in the mirror. If the agony of change takes me in the act of

writing this, Hyde will tear it into pieces. I pray and I hope that this doesn't happen, so my story can be told by its true teller. Lanyon was too sickened by what happened to write an accurate version.

Indeed, the doom that is closing in on both myself and Hyde has already changed and crushed him. Half an hour from now, I will again become the monster. I know that he will sit here, shivering and weeping in my chair. Will he be captured and punished? As Jekyll, I no longer care what happens to Hyde, but I do wonder about it.

This is my true hour of death. Hyde will take over my soul and I will never again grace this earth as the good Dr. Jekyll. Here then, as I get ready to lay down the pen and seal my confession, I bid you good-bye, my dear friend. I hope you learn well from my misery. If that is all I can leave behind, it will be enough.

THE END

Glossary and Pronunciation Guide

alter ego *(ALL-tur EE-goh)* the opposite side of someone's personality; *p. 147*

blackmail *(BLAK-male)* force someone to give money or behave a certain way by threatening to reveal an embarrassing secret; *p. 22*

confidential *(kahn-fuh-DEN-chul)* private; secret; *p. 132*

conscience *(KAHN-shunts)* a person's sense of right and wrong; *p. 124*

deformed *(dih-FORMD)* unusually or improperly shaped; *p. 43*

dingy *(DIN-jee)* dirty, stained, discolored; *p. 14*

expose *(ik-SPOZE)* reveal; uncover; make public; *p. 46*

forged *(FORJD)* falsely made, such as an illegal copy of money, a painting, or a signature; *p. 20*

foul play *(FOWL PLAY)* violence, especially murder; *p. 102*

identity *(eye-DEN-tuh-tee)* a sense of who a person is and of what makes him or her distinct from others; *p. 142*

inherit *(in-HER-ut)* receive money or property from someone after that person's death; *p. 46*

inheritor *(in-HER-uh-tur)* a person who *inherits* something; *p. 116*

irresponsible *(ir-ih-SPAHN-suh-bul)* unable to behave properly or do the right thing; *p. 140*

laboratory *(LAB-ruh-tor-ee)* a room where scientists perform experiments (*lab* for short); *p. 46*

madman *(MAD-man)* a crazy person; *p. 58*

madness *(MAD-nus)* mental illness; craziness; *p. 124*

potion *(POH-shun)* a mixture of liquids; *p. 144*

pounds *(POWNDZ)* units of money used in Great Britain; *p. 20*

ransacked *(RAN-sakd)* searched in a rough or messy manner; *p. 63*

remorse *(rih-MORSE)* painful sorrow or guilt over having done something wrong; *p. 164*

sanity *(SA-nuh-tee)* clearness of mind; mental health *p. 123*

scandal *(SKAN-dul)* something that causes great embarrassment or disgrace; *p. 20*

snarled *(SNARLD)* growled; *p. 173*

solitary *(SAH-luh-ter-ee)* on one's own; without friends or companions; *p. 87*

standards *(STAN-durdz)* rules or models set up as a measure of quality; *p. 140*

transformation *(trants-fur-MAY-shun)* a major change from one shape or appearance into another; *p. 150*

voluntary *(VAH-lun-ter-ee)* done freely, by one's own choice; *p. 159*

About the Author

Robert Louis Stevenson was born in Edinburgh, Scotland, in 1850. He grew up a frail and sickly child.

Stevenson's poor health prevented him from taking up a career in law. He then turned to writing. He traveled around the world in search of a cure for his ill condition.

In the four years between 1883 and 1887, Stevenson wrote his four longest and greatest novels: *The Strange Case of Dr. Jekyll and Mr. Hyde*, *Kidnapped*, *The Black Arrow*, and *Treasure Island*.

Stevenson spent his last years with his family on the South Pacific island of Samoa. There, he continued to write until 1894, when he died at the age of forty-four.

VALUES IN ACTION ®

Illustrated Classics

Series 1

The Adventures of Tom Sawyer
Black Beauty
Gulliver's Travels
Heidi
Jane Eyre
Little Women
Moby Dick
The Red Badge of Courage
Robinson Crusoe
The Secret Garden
Swiss Family Robinson
White Fang

Teacher's Guide available for each series

Series 2

Adventures of Huckleberry Finn
The Adventures of Robin Hood
The Adventures of Sherlock Holmes
Alice's Adventures in Wonderland
The Call of the Wild
Frankenstein
The Hunchback of Notre Dame
A Little Princess
Oliver Twist
The Prince and the Pauper
The Strange Case of Dr. Jekyll and Mr. Hyde
Treasure Island

www.readingchallenge.com